STEP INTO READING®

STEP 1

D1466377

The Blue Wish

By Mary Tillworth

Illustrated by Jeffrey Conrad

Random House 🏠 New York

Dear Parent:

Congratulations! Your child is taking
the first steps on an exciting journey.
The destination? Independent reading!

STEP INTO READING® will help your child get there. The program offers
five steps to reading success. Each step includes fun stories and colorful art.
There are also Step into Reading Sticker Books, Step into Reading Math
Readers, Step into Reading Phonics Readers, Step into Reading Write-In
Readers, and Step into Reading Phonics Boxed Sets—a complete literacy
program with something to interest every child.

Learning to Read, Step by Step!

Ready to Read   Preschool–Kindergarten
• big type and easy words • rhyme and rhythm • picture clues
For children who know the alphabet and are eager to
begin reading.

Reading with Help   Preschool–Grade 1
• basic vocabulary • short sentences • simple stories
For children who recognize familiar words and sound out
new words with help.

Reading on Your Own   Grades 1–3
• engaging characters • easy-to-follow plots • popular topics
For children who are ready to read on their own.

Reading Paragraphs   Grades 2–3
• challenging vocabulary • short paragraphs • exciting stories
For newly independent readers who read simple sentences
with confidence.

Ready for Chapters   Grades 2–4
• chapters • longer paragraphs • full-color art
For children who want to take the plunge into chapter books
but still like colorful pictures.

STEP INTO READING® is designed to give every child a successful
reading experience. The grade levels are only guides. Children can progress
through the steps at their own speed, developing confidence in their
reading, no matter what their grade.

Remember, a lifetime love of reading starts with a single step!

Maryoku Yummy™ and related trademarks © 2012 Cloudco, Inc. Used under license by Random House, Inc. All rights reserved. Published in the United States by Random House Children's Books, a division of Random House, Inc., 1745 Broadway, New York, NY 10019, and in Canada by Random House of Canada Limited, Toronto.

Step into Reading, Random House, and the Random House colophon are registered trademarks of Random House, Inc.

Visit us on the Web!
StepIntoReading.com
www.randomhouse.com/kids

Educators and librarians, for a variety of teaching tools, visit us at
www.randomhouse.com/teachers

ISBN: 978-0-307-93005-7 (trade) — ISBN: 978-0-375-97005-4 (lib. bdg.)

Printed in the United States of America

10 9 8 7 6 5 4 3 2 1

A blue Wish
hops into the van.
Hop, hop, hop!

Bob drives the Wish.

Go, go, go!

The blue Wish meets
the Wish Sitters!

Ooka is first.

Ooka is blue.

Fij Fij is yellow.

Maryoku
is pink.

Maryoku is
the best Wish Sitter.

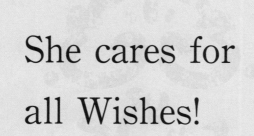

She cares for
all Wishes!

She hugs Wishes.

She feeds Wishes.

She gives
Wishes a bath.

She dances
with Wishes.

She makes
Wishes giggle.

And she twirls
with Wishes!

The Wish Sitters have
one big wish.

They want the
blue Wish
to be granted!

Ooka hugs

the blue Wish.

Fij Fij
waves
goodbye.

The Wish
Sitters have
made the
blue Wish
very happy.

The blue Wish

rises into the air.

Wishy-wish, Wishy-woo.
The little blue Wish
is coming true!